Perfect Odds

A Lucky in Love, Inc. Novelette

L.G. O'CONNOR

License Notes

Perfect Odds

A Lucky in Love, Inc. Novelette

L.G. O'CONNOR

Hi, I'm Olivia Yu. Ever ask, "What are the odds?" My business partner, Bach, and I do every day at Lucky in Love, Inc. We've built a multi-million-dollar business in three years, secretly engineering second-chance love for unsuspecting lonely hearts. Not bad for two Wharton B-school dropouts (unless you ask my parents, but that's another story.)

Sometimes it works, sometimes it doesn't. Either way, we take the odds. The next couple in our sights: airline flight attendant, Tanya Gates, and firefighter, Tate Manning. T & T. They sound cute, right? Too bad we have to give one of them the worst Valentine's Days ever to get this scenario to work. This time, when Bach says, "All it takes is one match," the sick f*ck means literally.

Chapter 1

"He's a famous surgeon. Good family..." Olivia Yu's mother chattered in rapid Mandarin, making another vain attempt at taking control of Olivia's pathetic love life. On today of all days, Olivia had no patience for her mother's guerrilla dating tactics.

Olivia held the cell phone away from her ear, half listening, as she shouldered open the glass door to her corner office at Lucky in Love, Inc. "Sorry, Mom," she said, interrupting her mother's diatribe. "I have another call. It's business. I'll call you later." She disconnected without a shred of guilt.

Her gaze zoomed in on a heart-shaped box of chocolates with a frothy red and black bow sitting on her keyboard.

Narrowing her eyes, she approached the large bank of high-definition screens behind her desk that flashed a multitude of Vegas and offshore odds spanning horse racing to sports games with a whole sector of niche betting in between, including theirs.

Her lips twitched up at the corners when she spotted the skull and crossbones pattern embedded in the black velvet covering the box like some gothic love parody.

She snickered softly and dropped her backpack on the floor beside her desk.

Sebastian cleared his throat behind her.

Olivia hid the remnants of a smile and cast a glance over her shoulder at the guy with a blond ponytail and golden stubble covering his angular jaw. Arms crossed nonchalantly over his chest, he leaned against the jamb, wearing ragged jeans, a black Nine Inch Nails hoodie, and a shit-eating grin.

"' Morning, Bach..." Olivia smirked.

Business partner and best friend, he'd earned his nickname from an uncanny resemblance to 80s rock icon Sebastian Bach. As good a way as any to make the most of having the same first name as that British kid who saved Fantasia in *The NeverEnding Story,* or the lead singer of Skid Row. Too bad the guy standing in front of her didn't believe in Luck Dragons and couldn't sing worth shit.

But what he lacked in whimsy and vocal cords, he made up for in brains and eye candy, though she'd never confess the last part. A healthy dose of ego came with all that pretty. And if it inflated any larger, he'd levitate like a balloon and slam head-first into the exposed pipes under their fifteen-foot ceiling.

Picking up the chocolates, she waved the box and said with more than a bit of sarcasm, "You shouldn't have," then tossed the gift on her desk. It landed with a *thunk* and slid to a halt halfway across the sleek Lucite surface. He understood how much she hated Valentine's Day and the loss it represented.

Five years had passed since Marcus's death, and every year since then, she and Bach had performed this dance. Olivia wanted to suffer in silence and let the day pass, and Bach wouldn't let her. Every year, he took great pains to flaunt convention. Last year, he'd chosen black roses with red, hand-painted spiders.

The holiday's irony wasn't lost on her. For them, every day was Valentine's Day in a business that made a crap ton of money betting on love. But the actual day represented something else entirely.

Sebastian strolled over and dropped his lean, muscled frame into one of her leather guest chairs. "Happy V-Day, Livvie." He knew better than to utter the actual V-word in her presence. Still, she couldn't figure out if it was the look in his eye, the bad boy smirk, or the British accent that made his statement sound like a venereal disease rather than a holiday.

He pointed to the discarded box, his blue eyes sparkling with amusement. "Come on! Open the damn thing. Those chocolates cost me a bloody fortune. I had special molds made. Twelve different poison bottles."

Olivia raised a brow but refused to break.

Rolling his eyes, he relented with a hangdog look. "They're your favorites. Dark chocolate with different liqueurs."

Damn him for resorting to chocolate. He knew her too well.

Olivia smiled, ripped open the wrapping, and removed the lid. Twelve finely crafted confections sat encased in purple tufted satin. She offered the first to Bach.

He waggled his eyebrows and selected the one in the center. A bulbous container marked "Hemlock" in Gothic script. She snatched the one that read, "Belladonna," and bit into it. Her mouth filled with raspberry liqueur, and she let out a throaty moan.

A dimple dented Bach's cheek when he smirked. "Did you just orgasm?"

"I might've," she teased and gave him a wink. "Next time, bring coffee. We've got work to do."

He chuckled. "Ingrate."

Olivia blew him a kiss. "It's nothing but love for you, baby." Then she logged into the system. "Let me pull the latest entries…"

Trepidation and excitement filled her veins as she downloaded the potential matches for their next love intervention and Lucky in Love play for the bookies in Vegas.

They needed to win big to make up for an unexpected hiccup during their last intervention that had decimated their cash reserves and ruined their perfect winning streak.

Sebastian slouched in the chair and cracked his knuckles. "How many submissions did we get?"

She pursed her lips and glanced at the file's row count. "Over three hundred." A healthy crop of heartfelt contest entries, stories of close friends or family members who deserved a second chance with the 'one who got away.' All for the cost of the ad and a $1,000 prize for the selected entry. *Thank you, Instagram.*

He let out a low whistle and plucked a bottle of "Arsenic" from the satin-lined box. "Nice. Spin them through the *algo* and see what Chess pops out," he said, referring to their home-grown AI agent.

"On it," Olivia said, and fed the file through an algorithm and the AI they'd developed to validate the entries and scrape the web to build comprehensive profiles on each potential couple, including every data point and social profile in digital existence to predict compatibility and receptivity, before winnowing down the options and identifying couples most likely to succeed…or not.

Either way, they were guaranteed a percentage of the *vig*—a cut of the charges for taking the bets—from the bookmakers. But the real money and the risk came from betting on the right outcome.

God, she loved this business model.

She and Bach had come a long way since that night in business school when they'd cooked up the idea for Lucky In Love, Inc., and their *One Who Got Away* game. All because Bach posed the question, "What are the odds she'll pick that bloke?" from his end of their ratty sofa while playing online poker as she indulged in a mindless night of television with her guilty pleasure, *The Bachelorette*.

The question triggered an all-nighter spent dissecting the elements of love. They concluded successful love matches boil down to receptivity, attraction, compatibility, and opportunity. They believed that if they could engineer the opportunity and predict the rest, then they could manufacture love. Better yet, they could monetize the outcome.

All they needed was live data, a proprietary algorithm, some AI, and a few good bookmakers.

Fast forward three years. Lucky in Love, Inc. had a net worth close to $100 million. More than enough value to satisfy and entertain a pair of twenty-eight-year-old Wharton MBA dropouts.

It had taken Olivia showing her traditional Chinese parents her bank balance after LIL's first year in business for them to forgive her for dropping out of one of the country's top universities to pursue her own business. Sadly, that hadn't stopped her mother from calling eight times a day on a quest to marry her off. Nothing like a non-stop litany of "I want a grandson before you turn into an old maid" in Mandarin to make your day.

Olivia's computer screen lit up with Chess's top ten highest-probability matches as Sebastian reached for another chocolate. Olivia slapped his hand and snatched the box from his grasp. "Hey! Stop poaching my poison."

His lips dropped into that pouty thing he did when making fun of her. "Sorry, lamb chop."

Insufferable wretch. Both vegan, he enjoyed needling her with meat endearments.

"Wow, really?" she deadpanned, then sent him Chess's results via a Slack message. "Here you go, turnip, your turn. Make it good." They never let the AI do all the work, always reserving the final decision for themselves and trading off on selections. She'd selected the last pair.

"A bland root vegetable. Is that the best you can do?" He scoffed, then scanned the dossiers on his phone while she checked email.

Twenty minutes later, a wicked smile twisted his lips, and he turned his screen to show her a profile. "This one."

Olivia read their names aloud. "Tanya and Tate. *Aww.* They sound cute." Their story had been submitted by Tate's mother. Olivia sat back in her chair and read the dossier she'd sent to Bach.

Now in their late thirties, Tanya Gates, a flight attendant, and Tate Manning, a firefighter, had met in high school. Olivia's gaze scanned their history and snagged on a connection to 9/11.

She swallowed hard and glared at Bach. Damn him, he'd picked them on purpose. He wanted her to invest. To care more than usual. To confront her demons. Blah, blah. God, she hated him sometimes.

Unblinking, Bach sat, fingers tented and silent, waiting for her to finish. She pressed on and checked the probability. "Wow, their scores are through the roof for compatibility and receptivity," she said, still irked but pleased with the numbers.

Bach gave a noncommittal nod.

Her gaze drifted to the inciting incident blessed by AI that would create the opportunity to reunite Tanya and Tate. She shot Bach another hard look. "A faulty toaster? Really?" If artificial intelligence ever took over the world, they were all screwed.

Bach's shit-eating grin returned as he leaned back in the chair, lifting the front legs from the floor. "All it takes is one match. The guy's a fireman, Livvie. Sometimes a spark isn't enough, you need a *flaaame,*" Bach said, making crazy eyes and wiggling his fingers like an out-of-control brush fire.

Olivia choked back an inappropriate laugh. "You're a sick fuck sometimes, Bach. Goes to show that video games *do* rot your brain." Since he wrote the damn algo and the LLM powering the AI.

Bach righted the chair and gave a smug smile. "That's why you fancy me." He blew out an exasperated breath at her unrelenting glare. "Oh, come on! Lighten up."

She didn't waver. "This is beyond risky. If we do this, no one gets hurt, and I mean *no one.*"

He rolled his eyes. "No one will get hurt, I promise."

"How do you know that?"

This time, Bach's gaze hardened. "Leave that to me. I wouldn't have made it an option if we couldn't control it."

She relented with a heavy sigh. "All right, but this scenario is going to cost us on the back-end to fund a rebuild. It better pay off. Big." This went beyond what they typically engineered, and she didn't love it. They'd be playing with fire. Literally.

"If we do this right, Spiro and his lot will set high enough odds to cover with just our cut of the vig, making the offshore bets gravy. It'll set us right after last time. What could go wrong?" he asked, unperturbed, stretching his long limbs like a languorous cat and lacing his fingers behind his head. With the move, his hoodie rose to expose a taut six-pack above the low-slung jeans.

She forced her gaze away from his abs and frowned. Catching her gaze, he smiled crookedly. "*Really?* What could go wrong?"

Did he seriously just ask her that?

Try as they might to engineer Fate—that wily bitch—occasionally rebelled and threw them an X factor, a variable so ludicrous their algorithms couldn't account for it.

Releasing a breath, he unlaced his fingers and straightened. The hoodie dropped into place. "No algorithm in the world could've predicted a rabid fox would bite the guy's dog and ruin the couple's evening. The chances of something like that happening again are like one in a bajillion," he said with a dismissive wave and a dramatic heavenward stare.

She sulked, wanting to believe him. "That's a bogus statistic."

He huffed a laugh. "Maybe. Just let it go."

Easier said than done. The rabid fox incident happened during her play and landed them in their current short-term financial crisis.

Clearly finished with the topic, he wagged his eyebrows. "What do you say to a little R&R in the Florida Keys when this is done?"

Olivia hid her surprise behind an expressionless glance, though the thought of escaping frigid New York City in mid-February for hot weather sounded enticing. "Us? *Together?*"

His face fell into a defensive scowl, and he shrugged. "Yeah, why not? We can rent a house on the beach."

That would be a first. Olivia couldn't deny the unexpected flutter in the pit of her stomach. She shook her head to clear it and mumbled, "OK…maybe." Then, she remembered his slovenly ways in grad school and gave him the stink eye. "If we do, I'm not picking up your dirty underwear."

He laughed, flashing more dimple. "I dare you to stop yourself. You're the most OCD person I know who doesn't have OCD."

She stuck out her tongue. "Ha, ha. And no parading around naked." He'd been shameless when they were suitemates. Probably because he had nothing to be ashamed of. She'd never quite gotten over that flash of full frontal after Marcus…She swallowed hard and suppressed the bittersweet thought.

Bach's smile went from smug to amused. "Only if you ask nicely."

A blush crested on her cheeks. She ignored his comment and circled back to their earlier topic. "I'm worried about this play."

He rocked forward and propped his elbows on her desk. His stare turned earnest. "This will pay off, Liv, and no one will get hurt. I promise," he said to soothe her.

Olivia avoided his gaze and scanned the report again. "Famous last words," she mumbled and reluctantly stood down. "Fine. I guess giving someone the worst Valentine's Day of their life is a small price to pay for finding true love. Get the team ready to deploy." They had fifteen hours—until midnight—starting now, to set up the scenario and have it play out with the unsuspecting couple.

Olivia ran the data through a second algorithm, one that turned their targets into avatars to conceal their true identities and added additional attributes and dramatic elements to make the game interesting, as well as to mask the true probability of success. These were the results they provided to the bookmakers.

The original algorithm was theirs and theirs alone. They used that one with its unfiltered probabilities to break the rules and place their offshore bets.

Spiro would kill them, literally, if he ever found out. If not him, a parade of mob-connected bookies behind him.

But that was the key to their business model. Love had a price, and that was their secret. Lucky in Love, not Las Vegas, was always the house.

Chapter 2

"Please turn off all laptops and electronic devices in preparation for landing. We hope you've enjoyed your flight. Have a safe and pleasant evening," Tanya said in the same smoky, sultry tone she used in her side hustle doing voiceovers. Back in high school when she dreamed of being the next Sade, her father used to say she had a voice that reminded him of fine whisky pouring over ice. Rest his soul.

Her throat tightened when she added, "Happy Valentine's Day." God knew someone deserved one, but it just wouldn't be her.

Gabriella belted herself into a jump seat and tittered, "You sound like a phone sex operator."

Tanya snorted, placed the intercom back on its hook, and mustered a cavalier bravado she didn't feel. "If I were, Gabs, at least I could loosely claim I had a sex life."

Gabriella smirked and tipped her head toward the cockpit. "Well, if that's all you want, Santos can't seem to take his eyes off your chest."

Tanya hadn't failed to notice the co-pilot's obsession with her *assets*. She'd heard enough rumors about him to pity his wife and three children. "That's a harassment charge, not a viable love match."

An aching sadness gripped her chest. Only working together for six months, Gabs had no idea how Tanya's life had imploded nine months ago, and what tonight should've meant for Tanya.

How her hopes and dreams had been shattered, her 'happy ever after' ripped away and given to someone else.

No, the love she had wanted would be on his way to Hawaii tomorrow morning with his new wife, on a honeymoon that should've been hers.

One saving grace, if there was any at all, she'd been saved an agonizing reminder that the father-daughter dance had represented.

"So...No plans for tonight, then?" Gabriella asked.

"Nope," Tanya said softly, and flashed a tight smile she hoped wasn't a grimace, "No plans."

Gabriella's expression brightened. "Come out with me and my girlfriends tonight! We're doing a pub crawl in Hoboken."

Tanya shook her head. "No, thanks. I'm exhausted. I could sleep for a week." And going out with a bunch of women a decade younger than herself would only depress her.

Spending time in bars was one of the things Tanya liked least about returning to single life. That, fix-ups, and dating apps. She'd hoped those things would be behind her as she approached forty. And they had been. For six years.

None of them were on her agenda for the next two days—a rare weekend off. She planned to spend her time binge-watching Netflix on her new couch, wearing flannel pajamas.

If she was lucky, she'd have just enough energy left to pick up an incredible Arturo's pizza and a bottle of Chianti on the way home.

Tanya made one last pass down the aisle to check on her passengers and collect any last-minute trash before taking her jump seat beside Gabriella.

In the hushed silence on the final descent into Newark airport, Tanya stared out at New York City's twinkling skyline. The Freedom Tower stood high and proud in the night sky, pinholes of light traversing the structure from the windows and the red blinking light at the apex.

A bittersweet lump rose in Tanya's throat, and she touched the cool window with her fingertips, reaching toward the living memorial that marked her father's grave and the others who perished there on 9/11.

I miss you, Daddy…Happy Valentine's Day.

Chapter 3

"Yo, Manning! 'S'up?" Gunner said as he entered the Maplewood, New Jersey, fire station and offered Tate a fist bump. Gunner's platoon started to roll in, adding to the flurry of activity in the firehouse as they prepared to take over when Tate's team came off their 24-hour shift.

"It's been quiet, too quiet. Know what I mean?" Tate said, hoping he wasn't cursing them with a last-minute call. He couldn't wait to reacquaint himself with his pillow and enjoy the next 72 hours off the clock. He had rooms to paint, a spare bathroom to renovate, and a damn squirrel to trap.

The little guy had made some recent late-night visits inside the rafters over his bedroom, and Tate had yet to find out how the squirrel had gotten inside. He suspected the oak tree that overhung his home like a giant umbrella played a role in the little guy's escapades.

Gunner gave a crooked smile and glanced at his watch. "Still an hour until eight. Never know what can happen," he said, walking by and heading toward the chatter in the upstairs kitchen.

Tate moved deeper into the garage and tucked himself between two fire engines, hoping for some privacy to make a call.

He hated Valentine's Day almost as much as he hated his ex-wife. It had been three years to the day when she'd pissed on their marriage. Nothing says, "I love you," quite like, "I'm leaving you for my personal trainer and taking half your net worth." He'd always link this holiday to her betrayal.

But one person in his life adored it, and for her, he'd make the effort regardless of how he felt.

His mom answered on the second ring. "Tate, honey! Happy Valentine's Day."

"Happy Valentine's Day, Mom," he said, his lips turning up.

"Thank you for the beautiful flowers, sweetheart. You are so thoughtful," she said, sounding as delighted as she did every year when his bouquet of red tulips arrived.

A tradition his father had started and Tate continued since he was seventeen, after his father died in 2001 on 9/11. Widowed at forty, his mom had never remarried. Now in her mid-sixties, she had a high-powered career as a financial services executive and could take care of herself. But as an only child, Tate felt responsible for looking after her.

Something his greedy ex-wife had resented, no matter how nice his mom had been to her.

"I'll pick you up at noon on Sunday," he said.

"You sure you won't come to church with me?" she coaxed.

Tension invaded his jaw, but he managed a polite reply, "Not this time." Unlike his mother, his faith died with his father in the World Trade Center collapse.

"Got to run."

"Before you go, honey, did you catch that squirrel yet?" Her curiosity held a hint of concern for the squirrel. She was a staunch believer in the 'catch and release' method, even for bugs. Not that he would ever harm an animal. Nope. He'd find the squirrel new digs in Memorial Park.

He sighed and rubbed his temple. "It's on my agenda for tomorrow." He hoped there were no early morning skirmishes over his bedroom before then. He needed some sleep. Who knew the damn things could make so much noise?

His mother laughed softly. "It could very well be a *she*. Mating season started this month."

Oh, joy. At least someone was getting tail back at the house. He gave a mirthless laugh. "Noted. See you Sunday."

As Tate headed to the stairs, an alarm tone pierced the air, and his personal radio crackled at his side with a call from dispatch.

So much for a quiet night.

The good-natured ribbing in the kitchen above him abruptly stopped. Chairs scraped across the floor, followed by the thunder of heavy footfalls as Tate's team rushed downstairs to gear up for their last call.

Tate joined them, and in less than a minute, the garage bays emptied. A fire truck and two engines peeled out with sirens wailing on their way across Maplewood to put out a residential fire.

"What the…?" Tanya Gates muttered. Her stomach clenched at the sight of emergency vehicles, red and blue lights spinning, jammed into the parking lot of her condo complex.

"Uh…Is that where you live?" asked the hipster Uber driver with trepidation as he pulled up to the temporary wooden blockades marked "Maplewood Police Department."

Tonya gulped, speechless, her gaze glued to the high-pressure water arcing from the fire hose to the flames licking through the second-floor windows of her townhouse.

"This can't be happening," Tanya muttered. Tears welled in her eyes, blurring her vision.

Silly her, thinking her day couldn't get any worse after finding her car's flat tire in the employee parking lot. That and the wedding reminders were unpleasant, but this was unspeakable.

Too shocked to think straight, Tanya mindlessly grabbed her handbag and the small suitcase on the floor beside her.

The driver turned and gave her a concerned glance. "Are you going to be okay? Want me to take you somewhere else?"

She stared at the fire, transfixed, and whispered, "No…" Then she exited the car into the brisk, smoky night and slowly walked toward the mayhem, suitcase rolling behind her.

Several firefighters worked the blaze from a ladder truck, while others worked hoses and various duties near the other large red vehicles.

As Tanya drew closer, mouth agape, she noticed her townhouse was the only one burning. A testament to fireproofed walls, she guessed.

A portly police officer with kind eyes stepped between her and a fire engine where emergency personnel gathered. Her eyes watered with more than tears from a plume of smoke-filled air that smelled like a chemical campfire.

"Miss, you need to stay back," he said gently, blocking her path.

"That's my home," she whispered, watching water douse the flames.

He pointed to his squad car. "Come sit for a minute. Let me get your information."

She stared at him blankly. This couldn't be happening. Didn't he understand her sanctuary was collapsing before her eyes? Sit? She didn't want to sit.

He squeezed her shoulder through the wool coat she wore and gave her a gentle shake. "The paperwork will help you with the insurance company." He tipped his head. "Come…"

The officer's words passed over her, like water over rock.

She stood rooted, unyielding, her gaze trained on the smoke billowing from her home, and her knees weakened when the tragic realization hit her. Her photographs. The suitcase handle slipped from her fingers, and her throat tightened.

"No!" She wrestled free from the officer and ran blindly, lungs heaving, toward one of the fire engines pumping water.

"Miss!" the police officer yelled behind her.

Ignoring him, Tanya ran full tilt toward the closest firefighter. He turned as she skidded to a halt.

One glance into his handsome face and time collapsed in on itself. The shock of recognition buckled her knees. Even with the ginger beard and passing years, she'd recognize him with his red hair and piercing blue eyes anywhere. If he smiled, a dimple would dent his left cheek.

He stood before her like an angel answering a whispered prayer. More tears slipped from her eyes. If anyone in the world understands, it would be him.

"Pictures…of my dad…in the bedroom," she choked out, expending her last breath before her eyes rolled back and the ground rose to meet her.

Tate froze, staring in disbelief, as he caught the tall, willowy woman's gaze. He blinked, taking in her delicate features and long, elegant neck swathed in a silk scarf with a familiar airline logo.

He'd only seen that unusual combination of hazel-green eyes and warm, light-brown skin on one person in his life. On a girl he once loved. Someone he'd lost a long, long time ago.

His heart thundered, and blood pounded in his ears as recognition lit in her gaze. "Pictures…of my dad…in the bedroom."

Her words hit like a gut punch. "Tanya?" he whispered as she collapsed in a dead faint. Like his father, hers had been one of the 2,606 souls who perished in the World Trade Center on 9/11; the shared experience that had galvanized their friendship.

He lunged and caught her before she hit the pavement, then swept her into his arms. "I need an EMT!"

She felt small and weightless in his embrace. Cradling her to his chest, he ran toward an ambulance. An EMT met him halfway.

"Check for shock." Tate reluctantly laid her on a waiting stretcher. But not before he drank her in, memorizing every detail. "Take good care of her… she's a friend. I'll be back."

Then he jogged toward the fire truck and the Battalion chief. "I'm going back in," he said, slipping his mask over his face.

His captain glared. "Like hell, you are, Manning! Wait until they finish knocking down the fire," he said, but Tate was already moving.

Tate knew it was stupid and reckless; he should have waited for the secondary sweep, but he understood, like no one else, what she'd lost. If those photos weren't protected by a door, they'd be as good as gone…if they weren't already.

The guys from the engine company were still fighting the blaze upstairs as he entered the charred first floor.

The point of origin had been an appliance in the kitchen.

A toaster.

There didn't seem to be any evidence of arson or accelerants, but he'd leave that to the investigators. Either way, the situation was almost under control. If he was lucky, the open flames would be out by the time he hit the second floor.

Tate took the stairs two at a time and caught up with the hoses in the smoke-filled hallway. Any visible flames had been extinguished when he reached the main bedroom.

"Hey, what are you doing up here?" One of the guys asked over the intercom.

"Trying to save something important," he said, and entered the bedroom. He did a visual sweep of the soot-stained walls and charred furniture. Smoke obscured his visibility, but he could make out the dresser, searching there first.

A few framed photographs were among the remains. Soot covered the cracked but intact glass. Tate couldn't see the pictures inside but snatched them anyway. He examined the other surfaces, then headed toward the closet. He checked the door first to eliminate unwanted surprises. None were waiting inside the ample walk-in space.

The contents inside were smoke-damaged but untouched by fire.

He shined the beam of his flashlight methodically around the closet, along the shelves over the hanging clothes, and then underneath until he spotted two brightly decorated photo boxes. He grabbed boxes, carrying them with the dresser photographs. One last sweep over the plastic tubs in the corner turned up nothing relevant. Satisfied, he left the way he came in.

The guys assigned to the secondary search and overhaul headed inside as he exited the front door. He slipped off his face mask and proceeded toward the ambulance.

He still couldn't believe it was Tanya. How long had it been, anyway? Almost twenty-five years since he'd met her at Montclair Academy, their private high school, during grief counseling for kids who had lost parents on 9/11? Over twenty years that she'd left for L.A. to try her hand at a singing career, and he had headed to Notre Dame on a football scholarship?

He hadn't wanted to lose her…They'd promised to stay in touch, visit, not stop…loving each other. Promises kids couldn't hope to keep with time and distance working against them.

Emotions stirred things inside him that he hadn't felt in longer than he cared to admit. Tanya had understood him down to his soul. No one had ever come close since.

And here she was, living less than a mile from his house. How did that happen? *When* did that happen?

Tate rounded the back of the ambulance. Tanya glanced up from where she sat on the stretcher, looking shaken but all right.

"She's fine," the EMT said with a wink and stepped away, giving them some privacy.

Tate's gaze locked on Tanya's, and he drew in a nervous breath. The boxes suddenly felt awkward in his hands. She was even more beautiful now than she'd been when they were teenagers.

He cleared his throat and said the first thing he thought of, "This is all I could find."

Her brows furrowed, and her hazel gaze slid to the boxes with the charred frames balanced on top. She bit her quivering lip, nodded, and held out her hands.

He had a million questions racing through his mind. Leading the pack, *"Why did you break our promise?"*

Chapter 4

The boxes and soot-covered photo frames shook in Tanya's hands. Tate stood before her, looking unsure of what to do with his hands, a tentative and assessing look creasing his brow.

Tate had recovered her pictures. Most of them, anyway.

Her favorite, the one she kept beside her bed, was missing. A photo with her dad after her professional musical debut as Cosette in Les Misérables at the Paper Mill Playhouse. A close-up portrait with their heads touching, highlighting their matching smiles and hazel-green eyes that captured her proud and perfect moment.

Taken a month before he perished, she never imagined that photo would be their last. Even with its loss, gratitude welled inside Tanya.

"Thank you," she rasped, but still not trusting her eyes, she swallowed hard and asked, "Tate? Is it really you?"

A look of relief washed over him. He nodded and dropped to one knee so they were at eye level. A small smile lifted the side of his mouth, a dimple denting his ginger-bearded cheek. "Yeah, it's me."

Lifting the boxes from her hands, he placed them carefully on the ground, removed his gloves, and dropped them alongside the boxes. Slowly, he cradled her hands in his. "Is there someone you'd like me to call...?" He hesitated and cleared his throat, "A husband, maybe? Or your mom?"

She shook her head, avoiding his gaze and thinking only briefly of her broken engagement. "I live alone...Mom's in Arizona now." Calling her mother before tomorrow was out of the question. She'd never get through a conversation without shattering into a million pieces. Not tonight.

"Hey..." He squeezed her hands, surrounding and warming them with strong fingers and rough palms, the palms of a man who worked with his hands. She found that comforting somehow. "Tanya? Look at me."

She met his earnest blue gaze. The intensity sent a flutter rippling through her middle.

"Do you need a place to stay tonight?"

She bit her lip, and a tear slid down her cheek. She nodded and dipped her chin. Any plans to slip into flannel pajamas and binge-watching Netflix were a distant memory.

Releasing a hand, he brushed away a tear with his thumb, sending a shiver over her skin, and said softly, "You can stay with me then."

Her head jerked up. "What?" They hadn't seen each other in years, and he was offering her a place to stay? "I-I can't let you do that," she stammered.

"Yes, you can," he said, his jaw set in a determined line. "I have a guest room. It's not a problem. Really."

She'd heard through a friend that he'd gotten married to his college sweetheart. He could have a whole brood of children by now. "I don't want to impose on you and your...family."

He laughed softly. "Divorced. No family to impose on." Relief and veiled excitement sparked inside her as he fished a key ring out of a pocket on his turnouts and removed a key. Pressing it into her palm, he closed her fingers around it. "Take it. I live five minutes from here. 25 Highland Place. You shouldn't drive. Want me to get you an Uber?"

No need to mention her stranded car and the flat tire. She nodded, at a loss for anything else to say. The key warmed her closed fist. "Thank you," she whispered.

A pretty, petite Asian woman in her mid-twenties with pink-tipped hair walked up wearing black jeans, combat boots, and an expensive fur-trimmed parka. "Sorry to bother you," she said, and extended a gloved hand. "Hi, I'm Liv."

Tanya tentatively shook it, surprised at the woman's firm grip, while Tate rose to his feet.

Liv pointed around the corner to another set of townhouse units, "We're neighbors. I just moved in. I'm so sorry about your home...I didn't mean to eavesdrop, but I'd be happy to give you a ride over to Highland. I'm running into town to pick up a pizza. It's no bother." She flushed and put a hand to her mouth. "I hope that doesn't sound weird…I just want to help."

Something about the tiny woman's self-deprecating demeanor disarmed Tanya and immediately set her at ease. It was nice to finally meet someone in her complex, even under dismal circumstances.

Picking up the boxes with the frames resting on top, Tanya smiled softly and rose from the stretcher where she'd been sitting beside the ambulance. "Thanks. I'd appreciate that."

Tanya had never seen Liv before. Not surprising. Tanya had only moved in three months before and had barely been home since she'd closed on the sale. She'd yet to meet any of her neighbors beyond friendly waves in the parking lot.

Tate eyed Liv with caution. "What unit did you say you lived in?"

Liv smiled broadly. "46G," she said, and pointed to the silver vehicle on the other side of the police barrier, "That's my Range Rover." She winked at Tate. "You can take down my plate if you're worried."

Tate eyed her warily and nodded with a tight smile, seemingly satisfied, then turned to Tanya. "I'm rolling off shift. I'll pick up something for us to eat on my way home from the station. In the meantime, my house is your house. Make yourself at home. I mean it…"

His warm, protective gaze roamed over her, as if to make sure she was stable on her feet. "Towels are in the closet beside the upstairs bathroom if you want to take a shower. I'll be there in an hour or so."

Warmth spread through her like a comforting blanket. "Thanks, Tate."

He eyed her purse. "Can I see your cell phone?"

"I'll hold those," Liv volunteered cheerily. Tanya transferred her precious cargo to Liv, retrieved the cell from her purse, and handed it to Tate.

He keyed in some numbers and handed it back. "I programmed myself into your contacts. Just text if you need anything." He started to go, then turned back as if he had forgotten something. "It's great to see you again, T-Girl," he said softly, her long-ago nickname rolling off his tongue and sending her back in time.

Tanya drew in a deep breath, watching his tall, retreating form jog towards the nearest fire truck.

Everything felt so surreal. The fire. Tate.

How had Tate ended up a firefighter? She'd always expected to see him on the field playing for the NFL. Then again, it made sense. After his father died, he wanted to make a difference, and they'd both had the utmost respect for the emergency workers who'd sacrificed their safety, some, ultimately, their lives, to work the 9/11 pile looking for survivors and remains. Her father had worked for Cantor Fitzgerald and Tate's for Marsh & McLennan. In the end, neither family had much to bury.

Exhaustion hit her, along with hunger pangs. She hoped she could wait until Tate came with food. She needed the strength for a long night ahead, which would start with a call to her insurance company.

A parting glance at her smoldering home made her queasy.

She gave Liv a weak smile and took back her photos. "I have to pick up my suitcase before we go," she said, and glanced across the parking lot to where she'd abandoned it next to the police car.

It was gone.

Liv pulled up to the curb beside a brightly lit two-story Victorian home that looked like it had slipped off the pages of *Architectural Digest*.

Tanya's lips fell open, and she double-checked the address. Definitely number twenty-five.

Did he live here *alone*? This was no bachelor pad. The Victorian was stately and elegant, sided in tan clapboard with white trim. Gray fish-scale shingles hung on the peaks over the windows, while dentil molding and architectural fretwork accentuated the house in all the right places. Low boxwood shrubs surrounded a wraparound porch, and a tall, majestic oak tree overhung the house, completing the picture of suburban bliss.

Tanya grabbed the door handle.

"Good luck with everything." Liv gave a sly brow waggle. "Especially with that hunky firefighter."

Tanya blushed. "He's an old friend from high school...." With an inward cringe, she thought about how it ended. All her fault. Every bit of it. "I still owe him an apology. My track record with men is pretty bad."

Liv gave her shoulder a little nudge and smiled wide. "Wake up, woman! Did you see the way he looked at you? My money's on forgiveness." She winked. "Don't let me down."

Tanya's cheeks heated, and she couldn't hold back a grin. "Thanks for the ride. It's really nice to meet you," she said, her words heartfelt.

As for Tate, she hoped Liv was right. Though she'd been around the block enough times to know that life was never that simple. Tate had offered her a place to stay. That was all.

Clutching the precious cargo to her chest, Tanya approached the house and sighed.

She caught the stench of burning embers clinging to her clothes. A shower ranked number one on her priority list, even over food…until she remembered everything she owned was inside the stolen suitcase.

Her shoulders slumped. Literally, all she had were the clothes on her back and the memories cradled in her arms.

During dark times, she'd lived with less. During the lean years in L.A. after she'd broken out with her hit single, "I'll Carry You with Me." After she'd overextended herself financially, only to find out the contract she'd signed with the record label had lined everyone's pockets but hers. After she'd run through her inheritance to break the contract, paid off her debts, and cut new demos to move her career forward. But that never quite happened. She toured with some bands but never saw another record deal.

Ten years of her life were spent trying to keep the promise to her father before she walked away, disillusioned, and became a flight attendant.

Sadly, now the only time she sang was in the shower.

Tanya climbed the wide front steps. Juggling the boxes, she slipped Tate's key into the lock. The door opened with a soft click, and she walked into comfortably warm air. R&B music played over the built-in sound system, an effect both welcoming and unsettling.

Her cell dinged with a text. Laying her belongings on a small table inside the door, which had a small tray containing a pair of earbuds and loose change, she dug for her phone.

Looks like you arrived safely. Turned on the lights and music using my Home app. Didn't want you freaking out thinking someone was in the house ☺

Relief cascaded through her in a giant wave. Her shoulders relaxed, and she laughed softly before replying.

Thanks. I'd wondered.

He responded. *What do you like on your pizza? I'm stopping at Arturo's.*

Her stomach answered with a gurgle, anticipating one of their wood-fired creations. *Anything but peppers!*

You got it! See you soon.

Something warm fluttered in her chest. Still, she had to choke back discomfort at the intimate nature of her next request. *Mind if I borrow something to wear? My suitcase seems to have disappeared.*

Three dots appeared.

LOL, help yourself. Will call my buddy, he's a cop in Maplewood. Will see what I can find out about the suitcase.

Tanya smiled despite herself. *Thanks!*

As Tanya tucked her cell phone inside her purse, she caught a flash of gray in her peripheral vision as it dashed around a corner and disappeared into the room on the left.

Tanya's mood brightened. A cat? Tate hadn't mentioned he had a cat. She must've startled the poor thing. As much as Tanya loved animals, she traveled too much to own a pet.

She kicked off her heels beside the entry table, padded across the shiny hardwood floor, and wandered after the animal into what turned out to be a richly appointed living room that included modern art, inset lighting, and an Oriental rug.

Tanya's brow rose, impressed. Her home had been cozy but, at her pay grade, much more Ikea.

Then again, Tate always had fine taste even back in high school. Wasn't he the one who helped her pick a new duvet set and repaint her bedroom to cheer her up when they'd first met?

Masculine and functional, the room had a massive flat-screen television that hung over the fireplace mantel, with a plush dove-gray sectional arranged for perfect viewing. In front of it, a square coffee table made from a highly polished slab of burled wood on an iron stand. A basket of remote controls, a bowl of mixed nuts, a nutcracker, and randomly scattered coasters with navy blue Giants logos sat on top.

She picked up a coaster and wondered again why Tate didn't go pro after college before chastising herself. *Maybe you'd know if you hadn't abandoned him all those years ago.*

She sighed, buried the regret, and wove her way through the dining room, where neatly piled tarps and paint cans sat in a corner. A work-in-progress compared to the living room.

No sign of Tate's feline companion, Tanya walked into a renovated kitchen and gasped. Now, she was downright jealous.

Painted in pearl gray with white maple cabinets and a matching island, the kitchen was a chef's delight with a Viking professional stove and a Sub-Zero refrigerator. Richly grained granite covered the countertops, and wide, gray-stained wood planks lined the floors.

A chill traversed her spine with the first uplifting thought she'd had since the fire: She'd rebuild her kitchen like this.

A chiming doorbell interrupted her reverie.

Expecting Tate, Tanya walked swiftly down the hallway and pulled open the tall door.

No one was there. Instead, outside the door sat a large package with a big red bow and an envelope with her name.

Brows furrowed, she cautiously approached the brightly wrapped box, pried off the taped card, and opened it.

No one's Valentine's Day should ever suck this much.
Liv & Your neighbors at The Commons

Chapter 5

"Are you out of your effing mind?!" Bach's exasperated voice boomed through the Bluetooth speaker in the rented Range Rover. Parked around the block from Tate's house, Olivia slumped lower in the seat and tried not to feel like a stalker.

Bach had blown a gasket when he'd found out she'd gone to Jersey, entered the play, and made contact with their targets.

Olivia ground her teeth, lowered the speaker volume, and hovered her finger over the disconnect button on the steering wheel, seriously contemplating hanging up on him.

"Liv, you're breaking every rule in the book! What the hell's the matter with you?"

"Don't get preachy," she finally snapped. What was one more broken rule? Their offshore bets would do more to land them in hot water than her insertion into a play. "I was worried! We burnt someone's house down. Shoot me! I wanted to make sure she was all right." That was one of the reasons, anyway.

It had been a while since Bach had gone ape shit on her for something she'd done on a play. He'd get over it, he always did. But Bach's tight tone told her it might take a while this time.

An unintelligible growl preceded his words. "That's what we pay deployment and execution teams for, Liv! I can't believe you told her your *name*. And you left her a bleedin' package? Are you insane? What's so difficult to understand about 'no involvement with the targets'?"

Olivia pictured Bach's flushed face as he sat on his plush leather couch in front of a bank of monitors covering the betting pools and the live odds for every bookmaker taking some of the action. As the scenario unfolded between the couple, the execution team processed their observations and uploaded fresh data into the algorithms, which potentially changed the probability of success and the bookmakers' odds.

Of course, the team had spotted her. She hadn't been trying to hide. But they knew better than to record it or report it to anyone but Bach.

She and Bach had only two rules: stay out of the plays and don't get caught laying their own offshore bets.

Lucky in Love had already banked the first payout for Tanya and Tate reconnecting at the fire scene, upping their corporate coffers over a million dollars, but that paled in comparison to how much they had riding on the final outcome—a kiss before midnight.

Today of all days, she wanted Tanya and Tate's happiness as much as she needed that juicy payout. Hence, her flagrant disregard for the rules.

"That's the second time you've questioned my sanity in one phone call," Liv said to the lunatic who'd programmed a fire scenario into their algorithm and the AI who blessed it. A sexy, lovable lunatic, but still a freaking lunatic. They were getting nowhere. She should've never answered the phone. Just wait until she told him what she'd snatched from Tanya's apartment before the team had arrived. Then he'd really question her mental health.

"And you still haven't answered me!" he snarled.

Heat traveled along her neck. "And I don't plan to!"

Bach's frustration was palpable. "We're not the only ones with eyes on this. What do you think Spiro will do if he catches wind of it?"

Something she didn't want to think about. Okay, fine. Bach had a point. Regardless, she pouted and changed the subject. "Why did you call anyway?"

He released a breath. "For the love of Pete, don't change the bloody subject!"

She dug in her heels, her tone frosting, "Why did you call?"

He swore again and sighed. "I wanted to make sure you were...all right."

Crap, here it comes. "Why wouldn't I be all right?" she asked, swallowing hard, not wanting to discuss it. The second reason she sat on her ass running surveillance when it wasn't her job. Plain and simple, she needed a constructive distraction.

His voice softened. "You know why."

She played dumb. "I do?"

He blew out a defeated breath. "Come on, Liv. I called because…I was worried about you."

Five years later, and it still gnawed at the center of her chest. The mugging, Marcus collapsing in a pool of blood, and dying in her arms on Valentine's Day.

"I'm fine, really," she lied, then waded into Bach's personal shark-infested waters. She wasn't the only one with steamer trunk-sized baggage. "What about you? How are you?"

He met her question with silence.

"Bach?"

Nothing but a deep exhale. "Stop deflecting. This isn't about me," Bach said finally. "Leave Jersey and come back to the city…Come to my flat." His voice carried a familiar ache, the one he got when he tried taking care of her. From anyone else, it would feel too close to pity, but not from him. Not tonight.

Despite all the innuendos they traded, they'd never come close to crossing the line. Besides, she'd been a hot mess since Marcus died, and then there was Bach's unending parade of women to avoid his pain. On paper, they weren't well suited. Regardless, he'd always been there for her. No matter what. And she for him.

In reality, her feelings for Bach were complicated. Not to mention her strict 'don't shit where you eat' policy. Like it or not, their livelihood depended on it. And in truth, even dead, Marcus still occupied a big part of her heart. But more and more lately, Bach's pull on her grew.

"I can't," she whispered. "Thanks. I'll call you later." She hit the end call button on the steering wheel before he could reply.

She may not get a happy ever after tonight, but she damn well wanted to give one to Tanya and Tate.

She checked the GPS tracking app on her phone. Tate's car was still parked at the firehouse. Screw it, she'd circle back and monitor this scenario from a visual distance. What else did she have to do?

Her phone rang. She checked the caller ID. Her mother. *Oh, hell, no.* She sent it to voicemail.

Bach called back. She let it ring. He called again.

Again.

Again.

She parked two houses down from Tate's, far enough away from the surveillance van, and killed the lights. Circumventing Bluetooth, she answered on Bach's fifth attempt.

"What?!" she whisper-hissed into the phone.

"About fucking time! Since you've inserted yourself into the surveillance, did you think to tap into the camera feeds lately?" he ground out, thoroughly pissed off.

What was the point of that? Tanya was alone. Rather than answer, she sniped, "We have people for that, as you recently reminded me. Why?" Couldn't he just let her stalk in peace and play Candy Crush until Tate arrived?

"You're not going to bloody believe it," he gritted.

"What?" she asked, her annoyance turning to apprehension.

"We have an X factor," he said.

The hairs prickled on the back of her neck. Was he serious? God, this couldn't be happening.

She counted to five and calmly asked, "Can we adjust the bets?" The payouts would grow in inverse proportion to the likelihood of success. A massive payout for anyone who beat the odds and bet the kiss would happen, but a huge loss for the same bets if it didn't.

"Too late, we're locked. We need that damnable kiss by midnight or we'll be living on gluten-free noodles for the foreseeable future." His voice held an edge of panic.

Shitballs. Olivia checked her watch. Three hours until midnight. Plenty of time to eliminate a threat. Taking a deep cleansing breath, she rubbed her forehead and asked, "What is it? Please don't tell me it's another rabid fox."

"Close. There's a bloody goddamn squirrel in the house."

She almost laughed. "Really? Is it rabid?"

"Doesn't look like it, no. Must have gotten in since we set up the cameras."

"What are we going to do?"

"I can't believe I'm actually saying this," he said, and growled with frustration. "The team needs your help."

Her brow furrowed. "My help? Why do they need *my* help? Do I look like I know anything about freaking pest control?"

He blew out a breath and seemed to regain his patience along with his cool. "Please, Liv. Just go meet Jeff. He'll fill you in."

Pressing her eyes shut, she sighed and hoped she wouldn't be sorry. "Fine. I'll call you later…And Bach? I have a feeling you're going to owe me big time for this one."

He snorted a laugh, "At this rate, I may have to pay you in trade."

"Swine." She hung up and did her best to ignore the warm tingles filling her nether region at the thought of a trade payment from Bach.

"You want me to *what?*" Olivia sat in the surveillance van across from Jeff and Tim, their execution team, and stared at them, incredulous. To quote Bach, had they lost their effing minds?

Jeff held up his hands in an attempt to reason with her. "The trellis on the back of the house is a no-go for us, but it could easily support your weight. It's attached to a lower roof, a clear path to the second-floor windows."

Her gaze bounced between the two men — one with a cast on his left leg and the other who tipped the scales well over three hundred pounds — and she scowled.

"Given that inane logic…sure, why the hell not?" she said, her voice dripping with sarcasm, and threw up her hands. "You seriously expect me to scale the side of the house on a rose trellis, crawl in through a second-floor window, bag a frightened squirrel, and escape — with the squirrel! — unnoticed?"

They nodded in unison and dared to crack enthusiastic smiles.

"*Bèn dàn,*" she muttered. The Mandarin equivalent of idiot. "Are you both crazy? Do I look like I specialize in breaking and entering? That's what we pay you for!" She glared, wiping the stupid grins off their faces. "How do you expect me to catch this thing? With my bare hands?"

Jeff held up a finger, then rummaged in one of the storage lockers and pulled out a small dart gun with a cassette of multi-sized cartridges. He loaded the smallest cartridge into the chamber and offered her the dart gun with a self-satisfied look.

"We added this to the toolkit after the fox disaster. Just nip the little guy with one of these. Takes about ten seconds to knock him out, then scoop him into the burlap sack. Should be easy."

"Ha! Easy for a professional," she grumbled and pointed to the monitors lining the van's interior. Tanya was upstairs in the guest room beside where the squirrel had temporarily taken refuge inside a closet. "She's too close. How are you going to distract her?"

Tim opened the costume trunk and pulled out a policeman's uniform, a utility belt with everything, including a sidearm, and a radio. "Leave that to me."

They were good, she'd begrudgingly give them that.

She rolled her head back to stare at the van's roof for a second, then took a deep breath and snatched the dart gun. "I can't believe I'm doing this," she muttered.

Olivia's heart pounded as she jimmied open the unlocked second-floor window and gingerly stepped into the sparsely decorated guest room.

"Sweet Jesus, I'm in," she muttered. The night vision goggles were badass, but the headgear made her feel like a coal miner.

Their furry four-legged friend could be anywhere among the butt load of unpacked boxes, folded tarps and paint cans that surrounded the bed and small dresser. It looked more like a storage room than guest accommodations.

She lowered the window and crept farther inside. Not wanting to fry her retinas, she avoided glancing through the goggles at the slim, blinding shaft of light that filtered in through the slightly open bedroom door.

"Where is it?" Olivia whispered.

"Still in the closet," Jeff said through her earpiece.

In the bathroom on the other side of the wall, she heard the rustle of makeup and Tanya singing along to a Sade tune that played on the sound system. Tanya's pitch-perfect voice sent a shiver down Olivia's spine. That girl could sing.

You better do right by her, Tate, Olivia thought. Not to mention, make this squirrel hunt worth it.

"You there?" Jeff asked, pulling her back.

"Yup." Olivia shucked off the backpack, unzipped it, and removed the dart gun. The downstairs doorbell rang.

Officer Tim, right on time to return Tanya's stolen suitcase, the one Liv pilfered to ensure Tanya wore the eye-popping present she'd left on the porch. They needed that kiss.

Tanya's footsteps receded and then echoed down the wooden staircase.

A scratching sound came from inside the closet.

"He's in there," she whispered.

"Whatever you do, don't spook the little guy. They can shred the place in no time."

Olivia rolled her eyes. Like she didn't know that?

As Tanya exchanged a few words with Tim downstairs, Olivia crept to the closet and peered inside.

The squirrel froze with a peanut clasped in its tiny paws.

Just as Olivia aimed the dart gun, the squirrel let out a squeak, dropped the nut, and leaped out of the closet. In a fluffy blur of tail, the squirrel dashed out the open bedroom door and into the hallway.

Mandarin curses flew from Olivia's mouth that damned not only the rodent's mother but its entire bloodline.

"Abort! I repeat, abort!" Jeff hissed through the earpiece.

Chapter 6

Wine bottle tucked beneath an arm, Tate balanced the hot pizza box and dug for the spare key hidden inside the potted shrub at the base of the front steps.

His pulse quickened at the thought of seeing Tanya. "I must be out of my damn mind," he muttered. Inviting her here had seemed like a good idea in the moment, but he hadn't really thought it through.

But she needed him, right? That's what mattered.

Old bullshit could wait. Yet once the shock had worn off, it's all Tate had thought about since stepping into the shower at the firehouse. How she'd let him down, then disappeared from his life without a trace… until tonight's fire.

He keyed open the lock and walked in. Over the R&B music — Tanya's favorite — he heard her engrossed in conversation on the phone upstairs.

Not wanting to disturb her, Tate headed down the hall to the kitchen. He didn't envy her the hassle of dealing with the insurance company or sifting through what remained of her burned and smoke-damaged possessions.

Footsteps descended the front stairs as he placed the wine on the granite-topped island and rested the pizza box on the stove.

"Hey," a familiar sultry voice said from behind him, sending an unexpected shiver over his skin straight down to his groin. Damn. All these years later, the sound of her voice still unwound him.

He took a steadying breath and pivoted. "I hope you like mushroom and meatball on …" The words died in his throat. He blinked, once, twice. "Holy… You look… Amazing."

His appreciative gaze took in every detail—the heels, the slinky green sheath dress that matched her eyes and clung to her curves, all that smooth skin. She wore no makeup other than gloss on her full lips. Her spiral locks fell loose, taken down from an earlier bun, and touched her bare shoulders.

Holy. Wow. She looked like Naomi Campbell in her supermodel heyday. That, coupled with her incredible talent, had been the impetus behind her move to L.A. after high school to pursue a music career.

As he stood there gaping like an idiot, he remembered the missing suitcase. His brow creased. "Wait a second. That wasn't in my closet."

She glanced down at her outfit, and her lips twitched into an amused smile. "It wasn't. It was a gift from Liv and my neighbors at The Commons. They left it in a box on your porch. I'm shocked it all fit."

Thank you, Liv. Swallowing hard, he rebooted his brain with a mental bitch slap, pulled out a corkscrew, and reached for the wine. "Resourceful bunch. Much better than one of my T-shirts and my sweatpants." He chuckled. Truthfully, the thought of her wearing his clothes had the same effect on his blood flow as the dress.

He held up the wine bottle. "Drink?" God knew he needed one, if only to inebriate the jackrabbit tapping out River Dance in his stomach, and to rid the air of nervous tension.

She nodded, her shoulders relaxing. "Thanks for calling your friend. A police officer dropped off my suitcase."

His brows flicked up. Why hadn't his buddy let him know? "Really? That's great," he said, not thinking too hard about it. With a light pop, the cork slipped free of the bottle. He brushed his gaze over her again. "For what it's worth, that's a great dress."

Her smile smoothed the worry lines on her face, and for the first time all night, he saw his T-Girl again. "Thanks."

"I heard you on the phone. Insurance company?" he asked.

She nodded, pulling one of the stools from under the island, and sat. "I have an appointment with the adjuster tomorrow morning at ten." Then her lips curved up into a soft smile, and she met his gaze. "Thank you, Tate…for everything."

Warmth filled his chest, and he cleared his throat. "Did I get everything?"

Her smile faltered a fraction. "Most."

He frowned. "I missed something?"

She gave a shrug like it didn't matter, but after all these years, he could still read her tells — the quick glance away, the quirk at the left side of her mouth. "The one on my bedside table."

His frown deepened, and he shook his head. "I checked every surface, T. There weren't any pictures next to your bed. I promise." Losing his own father had been tough, but they'd never been as close as Tanya and her dad. "Does your Mom have a copy — ?"

She reached over, squeezed his forearm, and said softly, "It's all right. I'm so grateful for what you found." The touch of her fingers unlocked a familiar yearning for more.

He covered her hand in his, gave her a gentle squeeze, and slipped free of her grasp. He needed space between them, to get away from her gravitational pull before he did something stupid.

"Hungry?" he asked, feigning nonchalance, and moved across the kitchen to retrieve two wine glasses, plates, and some napkins. He pointed to the pizza. "One slice or two?"

She dispelled the tension with a little laugh. "Two. I'm starving."

That made one of them. Tate was too nervous to eat. He still couldn't believe Tanya was here. In his mind, she'd always been the one who had gotten away. And he still didn't know why…what he'd done for her to disappear like that. A question that's haunted him for more than twenty years.

If nothing else, he needed an answer.

He doled out the wood-fired pizza, took a seat beside her, and poured two glasses of Chianti. Offering her one, he held up the other. "Toast?"

Her gaze brightened, and she touched her glass to his.

Hoping he wasn't being too presumptuous, Tate said, "To old friends and new beginnings."

"I'd like that," she said, giving a tilt of her head and taking a sip.

The wine hit his tongue in an explosion of flavor. He downed half the glass before thinking better of it, and let his frayed nerves slowly settle.

They ate in companionable silence. He refilled their glasses and plates. The tension of unanswered questions rippled silently between them as he worked up the courage to address the elephant in the room.

When he looked at her, he still saw the girl who held him in her arms and sang to him softly during those dark days filled with survivors' sadness. He'd done the same for her. Out of their sadness came solace and a soul-deep friendship that turned into more. Inseparable, they spent almost a year together. He gave her his body and his heart, and when he left for Notre Dame, part of him stayed behind. With her.

He'd understood the root of her passionate drive to pursue a singing career more than anyone. It had been the one thing, besides him, that held her together back then. Yet, in his desperation, he tried to hold on to her.

He started slow and asked quietly, "Where've you been all these years, T? Why didn't you keep our promise?"

Where to begin? Tanya thought, letting out a soft sigh and pushing her empty plate aside. She stared into Tate's expressive blue eyes. Old pain and hurt stirred behind them and cut her to the core.

She couldn't believe she was here, in the kitchen of the boy, now man, whom she'd left that day. The boy who'd owned her heart from the moment she met him in their grief group. Staring into his eyes, she realized her soul had never stopped yearning for him, and he deserved an answer.

The last time he'd seen her was the day he'd left for Notre Dame, and she'd gone with her mother on their cross-country road trip to L.A. to pursue her dream.

Her throat tightened. She'd sacrificed her promise to Tate to keep another. She'd promised him that she'd give their long-distance relationship a chance.

At the time, she had no idea what it would take to keep the first promise she'd made...The one she'd made to her father, to pursue her dreams of a music career. She'd naively thought she could keep both.

What she hadn't counted on was how quickly the lifestyle she found in L.A. would devour her days and nights. Her calls to Tate grew less frequent, her letters shorter.

It all came to a head that first fall, Tate's freshman year at Notre Dame. She'd promised to visit him for the biggest football game of the season and stay the weekend, part of their plan to stay together while they both pursued their dreams.

Her eyes welled, and she opened her mouth to speak, but no words came.

He reached for her hand and wrapped it in warmth. His brow furrowed, his gaze penetrating, "I waited at the bus station for hours. You never showed up or returned my calls... I got the note a few days later. What did I do?"

The thought of Tate waiting and worrying...

Her tears spilled over, and she wiped them away with one hand as she squeezed his hand in her other. "You didn't do anything wrong," she whispered, "It was me."

He brushed his thumb across the back of her hand. "Tell me," he said softly.

She pressed on, ashamed at how she had handled things. "I had an audition a couple of days before I was supposed to see you. A producer for one of the record labels who represented a few big-name R&B bands heard my demo of 'I'll Carry You with Me.' One of the bands had an unexpected opening for a backup singer. The producer told me if I got it, I'd have the opportunity for a solo spot to crowd test the song."

He nodded, his gaze coaxing but unwavering.

She paused and slipped her hand from his before she continued. It didn't feel right to be touching him as she relived this. She stared at her lap and let the scene play out in her head. "They hired me on the spot. But they didn't tell me until I got there that I had to join the tour the next day, and that I would be gone for six months."

She paused, remembering the awful scene that night with her mother and her manager as she tried to persuade them to ask the producer to delay her start by a few days. Her insides had ripped apart over the decision as she'd clutched the bus ticket Tate had sent her, not wanting to choose between seeing him and the potential opportunity of a lifetime.

Tanya sighed. "My mom and I had a big fight. She said I had to choose...that if I passed up the opportunity, I'd resent you."

"Baby, I know you think you love that boy, but you can't fool yourself into thinking you can have Tate and this dream you're chasing. You need to focus on your music. Don't give up your dream for foolish promises you can't keep. Make your daddy proud."

Tate swallowed. "I would've understood. You didn't have to cut me out of your life." Anger tinged his hurt.

Her voice quivered, and she shook her head. "She was right. In my heart, I knew if I couldn't choose you, then I had to let you go. Not because I didn't love you, but because I couldn't put you first," she sniffed and wiped away a tear. "I didn't know how to tell you. Any of it. Then it was too late, so I sent the note..." How often she'd thought of that note over the years. Every cowardly word of it.

Forgive me, Tate. I'm so sorry for what I've done and for what I'm about to do. It's not because I don't love you, it's because I do.

There are places I need to go that you can't follow.

I'm giving you back your freedom and taking mine.

Not forever, but for now.

This isn't goodbye.

I promise.

I love you, Tanya

"My life went crazy after that. When I got back from the tour, I signed a record deal for 'I'll Carry You with Me,'" she said, giving him a sad smile. "But the song wasn't just about my dad anymore, it was about you, too." She placed a hand to her heart. "You've always been here, Tate. Even when I couldn't be with you, I've carried you with me."

Tears flowed freely down her cheeks. There were so many times she thought of Tate and what they could've had. So. Many. Times. When everything went wrong with the record company, she considered giving up on her dream and coming home. And she almost had...

A smile ghosted over his lips. "I remember when the song came out. I was so proud." Then a pained expression crossed Tate's face. "You said you'd come back, T."

She brushed her fingers down the soft wool sweater covering his arm. "I did..."

The muscles in his arm tensed under her touch. "What do you mean? I never saw you again."

The tears came faster than she could brush them away. "Christmas break, your senior year of college. You were home for the holidays with your mom." When they were still living in Montclair.

Tate frowned deeply and shook his head, his blue eyes burning. "What are you saying...?" he whispered.

She gave him a watery smile. "I was in New York City, on a 10-city tour with an R&B band. I worked up my courage and dropped by one night. I prayed that you'd talk to me. But you weren't home. You were out for the night with your girlfriend." She remembered her feelings of utter desolation, along with the guilt she felt over how she'd let him down.

Tate's jaw twitched, and his eyes misted. "I didn't know."

Tanya laid her hand on his. "That's because I asked your mom not to say anything. After what I'd done, I didn't have the right to disrupt your life. I was too late…That girl, she was the one you married?"

He nodded once and swept a hand over his face. "God, T., why didn't you tell me? Why didn't you trust me?" he asked with a hint of frustration.

"I'm so sorry. I never wanted to hurt you."

He passed a thumb over her cheek to wipe away the tears, and said, "I would've given anything to be with you." He looked as bereft as she felt.

His words cracked her wide open. "You had dreams, too, and I couldn't let you give them up." Had he been home that night and unencumbered, maybe things would've been different.

He stepped off his stool and pulled her into his strong arms, her head resting against his chest. His heart beat strong under his sweater. "But you were always meant to be part of those dreams," he whispered into her hair. "It's not too late. Give us another chance?"

Her heart stuttered in her chest. The tragedy of the fire faded into the background, along with the obstacles that kept them apart for all these years. This moment felt so much bigger. More important. Magical.

He reached down and tipped her head back so that she stared up into his eyes. Eyes filled with heat and longing.

She touched his cheek, his beard soft under her fingertips. Her gaze lingered on his full lips, and she nodded. Yes, she wanted that too.

But first, she needed to know. "What about you? Your football scholarship? The NFL?"

He shrugged and ran one of her curls through his fingers, his touch sending a shiver over her skin. "Bum knee from an injury during my senior year, so I came home after graduation. Opened a construction business and made a fortune during the housing bubble. Got divorced and lost half of that fortune. After that, I transitioned from voluntary to paid firefighting. I still do construction on the side."

His fingers moved from her hair to her cheek, his body pressed flush to hers. "I've missed you," he said, lowering his mouth.

Her heart soared as he came in for a kiss.

A loud crash in the living room halted Tate's descending lips.

She laughed softly. "Your cat has impeccable timing."

He pulled back, and his brow knitted in confusion. "What cat? I don't have a cat." Then his eyes widened. "Oh, shit!" He bolted for the living room.

She ran after him.

As they rounded the corner, he snapped on the light.

Sitting in the middle of the coffee table was a toppled bowl, scattered nuts, and a fluffy-tailed gray squirrel stuffing the bounty into its cheeks.

They all screamed at once.

Tate grabbed the blanket on the back of the couch, unfolded it, and held it out like a matador.

The squirrel dropped a peanut as Tate tossed the blanket. In a panicked dash, the squirrel leaped from the table to the back of the sofa, avoiding the falling blanket, and onto the floor. Tiny nails scrabbled on hardwood around a corner into the front hall.

Oh my God, she needed to get her eyes checked. How did she mistake a squirrel for a cat?

Blanket in hand, Tate swore and leaped over the back of the sectional. "You okay?"

Heart pumping, she nodded and slipped off her heels.

"We need to trap that little bastard and get him out of the house before he destroys the place," Tate said with a determined set to his jaw.

"I'll try not to scare him this time," she promised, following Tate in stocking feet.

Another crash sounded upstairs. Tate opened the front door as they passed, letting in a chilly gust of air. "We'll flush him out if we can't catch him," he said.

She followed Tate, who took the stairs two at a time.

He pointed to the right when she arrived. "You go that way, I'll go this way. If you find him, call me and trap him in whatever room you find him in. OK?"

She nodded and headed into the open guest room where she'd left her things. Nothing was disturbed, so she checked the bathroom where she'd taken a shower. Nothing. The closet door stood slightly ajar. She opened it the rest of the way and turned on the light. A pile of empty nutshells sat in the corner, and above it, a hole chewed through the ceiling from the attic. Well, that explained how the squirrel got into the house.

A blur of gray fluff flew by the bedroom doorway with Tate on its tail.

She followed them, grinding to a halt behind Tate, where he'd cornered the petrified animal in an unfinished bedroom.

"Tate, honey! Are you home?" A mature female voice boomed from downstairs.

"Christ on a bike," Tate muttered. Holding the blanket in front of him like he was blocking a pass, he turned to her. "T, it's my mom. I have no idea what she's doing here this late, but can you tell her I'll be down in a minute?"

The squirrel chittered in a distressed wail, clambered up the wall, and launched itself onto the ceiling fan.

"Please don't hurt the little guy," Tanya said.

He craned his neck and shot her a reassuring half smile. "Don't worry, T. I won't."

She closed the door and hurried downstairs.

"Mrs. Manning!"

Claire Manning stood inside the door with a gray-haired man at her side. They were both dressed for a night out on the town. A look of surprise on his mother's face shifted to delight. "Tanya, is that you?"

Tanya hadn't realized how much she'd missed Tate's mother. This Valentine's Day held both the best and the worst experiences she could've ever imagined.

Tanya rushed into the woman's arms and hugged her. "It's so good to see you again." Then she eyed the large wire contraption resting on the floor at Claire's feet. "What's that?"

"A trap. Tate told me he's having a squirrel issue. I'd planned to leave this on the porch until I saw the door wide open."

The stress of the day had finally caught up with her. Unable to stop her giggles, Tanya broke into laughter. Trying to catch her breath and speak at the same time, she held her stomach. "He has it cornered upstairs in the bedroom."

His mother's eyebrows rose, and she said dryly, "Is that why he's letting all the heat out of the house? I thought maybe he was getting robbed."

Tanya chuckled and wiped away mirthful tears. Mascara wasn't her friend today. "I'm sorry, it's been a stressful day." Tanya stared at the man and held out her hand. "I'm Tanya."

He smiled warmly and shook it. "Mike."

His mother grabbed the wire trap and started toward the kitchen at a fast clip. "Time for introductions later, we need to bait this thing."

Tanya headed to the living room for a handful of nuts, while his mother slathered a bunch of crackers with peanut butter. Then they headed to where Tate had bunkered down with the squirrel.

The creature dangled upside down from the ceiling fan, clinging on for dear life, when Tanya and Tate's mother slipped inside with the trap. Tate had the window wide open and stood nearby with the blanket. Mike had been reluctantly relegated to the living room to wait it out.

"Hey, Mom. What are you doing here?" Tate asked, then caught sight of the trap. "Sweet."

Claire propped open the cage door and arranged the squirrel bait inside. "Mike and I were on the way home from our date—"

Blanket still in hand, Tate's head snapped around. "Mike? Mike, who?"

She laughed softly and blushed. "Mike Garibaldi…he owns the hardware store downtown. We're dating."

Tate's brows popped up, followed by a look that could only be described as hurt. "You are? When were you going to tell me?"

"At brunch, on Sunday," she said, then cleared her throat and winked at Tanya. "I'm not the only one who's been holding out, am I? Why don't we leave our little friend here and take our chat downstairs?" Tate's mother smiled at Tanya. "I think we all have some catching up to do."

Inching out of the room, they closed the squirrel inside with the baited trap and joined Mike downstairs. Tate greeted him with familiar warmth. Turned out, Tate was a frequent customer at Mike's store.

Tate lit a fire, and they gathered on the dove-gray sectional. Wine in hand, they settled in and traded stories.

Tanya went first. She filled them in on her years in L.A., her hit single and ensuing lawsuit, her career change to become a flight attendant, and buying her home in Maplewood without realizing Tate and his mother lived only a few miles away.

Claire went next and regaled them with how she'd visited Mike's hardware store for years and how their long-standing flirtation had recently turned into a relationship.

Finally, Tate shared his story about purchasing his home, the ongoing renovations, and his immense pleasure at hosting his first official house guest.

Two hours later, Claire and Mike left with one extra passenger stuffed to the gills with peanut butter and mixed nuts. They planned to release the well-fed squirrel in Mike's backyard across town.

But before they left, Claire caught Tanya alone in the kitchen.

With misty eyes, she pulled Tanya in for a hug. "I'm so sorry about the fire, sweetheart. But you being here is like a blessing." When she'd released her, she brushed away a tear. "I've never forgiven myself for not telling Tate you came to see him that night."

Tanya released a heavy sigh. "I'm sorry I put you in that position."

Tate's mother smiled and squeezed Tanya's arm. "For Tate, you were the one who got away. Be gentle with his heart. He's a good man."

Tanya's throat tightened. "I know," she whispered. "I promise to do right by him this time."

"That's all I ask, honey."

After seeing them all off, Tanya and Tate returned to the sofa and snuggled in front of the fire.

A quick glance at the cable box revealed it was almost midnight. This truly had been Tanya's best and worst Valentine's Day ever.

Tate pulled her close and brushed a lock of hair from her face. "Where were we?" he asked, eyes sparkling and wearing a crooked smile. He traced her lip with a finger.

She shivered under his touch. "Am I forgiven just a little?"

"Only if you promise to make it up to me," he teased, then clasped her hand in his and brought it to his lips for a kiss.

Had it only been a few hours since her world tilted on its axis and she'd found Tate again? Whatever this was, whatever this could be, she wanted to give it the chance it always deserved.

It had taken her years of chasing her dream to figure out that it wasn't the music career her father wanted her to have as much as what it had represented—happiness.

"I promise that and more," she said. Bridging the gap between them, she cradled his head in her hands and kissed him in a dance of lips and tongue until everything receded and all that remained was the boy who'd pulled her from grief and stolen her teenage heart.

Chapter 7

Olivia made it to Bach's Upper West Side apartment building by 2 a.m. and slipped inside behind a couple too absorbed in a quiet conversation to notice her.

After the squirrel debacle and confirming their win, Olivia visited the fire scene. She slipped the beautiful photograph of Tanya and her father back where it belonged on top of the charred nightstand next to Tanya's bed, where she'd surely find it. Untouched.

Like Tate and Tanya, Olivia had lost someone on 9/11. Her grandmother, a kitchen worker at Windows on the World, died in the tower collapse of the north tower when Olivia was a toddler. One of Olivia's most treasured possessions was a picture of her sitting on her grandmother's lap. When Olivia had seen the surveillance footage inside Tanya's townhouse, she knew she had to save that photograph.

She nodded at the doorman manning the security desk. He eyed her with recognition as she passed, tipped his head, and smiled. Hanging back, Olivia waited for the elevator doors to close behind the canoodling couple and caught the next one.

She remembered nights like that in another life when she'd been with Marcus, and she wondered if she would always feel like an outsider looking in. But if that were true, why was she on her way to the 17th floor? She and Bach could easily tally their winnings tomorrow, but the truth was that she needed him — and only him — tonight.

The win hadn't been enough. Even under threat from their nut-loving little friend, they'd beaten the odds and won. She'd watched Tate and Tanya kiss less than five minutes before the stroke of midnight, but the rush she felt had fled by the time she'd driven through the Lincoln

Tunnel, leaving her aching for comfort that only one person could provide. Screw how much this could complicate things.

She pressed Bach's buzzer. The door cracked open less than a minute later, and a sleepy-eyed Sebastian greeted her wearing only pajama bottoms, his bare, chiseled chest on full display. "Liv?"

"Hi," she whispered, at a loss for anything else to say. But no words were necessary.

A lazy smile slipped onto his lips, and his blue eyes shimmered with a naked softness. He met her gaze with an array of emotions that sucked her breath away. Relief mixed with yearning and desire. The two things he'd never said aloud or acted on. Feelings she knew well and denied just as fiercely.

He reached for her hand and tugged her inside. She entered the darkness, and he led her to his bedroom. Stripping down to her underwear, she crawled into his bed after him. He wrapped his arms around her and spooned her tight to his body like he had so many nights. Tonight was different; she felt it deep in her soul. Tucked beneath the blankets, she let his warmth permeate her skin.

"How many times did your mum call today?" he asked quietly, his breath warming her hair.

She would've found the answer comical if the calls hadn't pissed her off so much. "Thirteen."

"Did she ask about Marcus even once?" His voice was an aching whisper.

Olivia's throat tightened. The cork popped on her bottled emotions and spilled over like wasted champagne. A sob broke free. "No…"

Of course, not. Marcus hadn't been a wealthy doctor from a good Chinese family. He'd been a British musician with a kind heart who'd loved her unconditionally—a thoroughly unacceptable choice by her parents' standards. If he had lived long enough to put the ring on her finger they'd found inside his pocket the night he died, her parents would've disowned her.

"He was my brother, Liv. I miss him, too…" Bach said gently, stroking her hair as she shook and her wails hit a crescendo.

Minutes passed. He held her tight, his chin tucked alongside her neck. After what felt like an eternity, she swallowed hard, completely wrung out of tears, and breathed his name. "Sebastian?"

"Yeah?"

"It's time we let him go," she sniffled.

"I know." His voice was a gentle caress.

Looking back, she realized Sebastian had been leading her to this moment for a long time. She was finally ready to embrace it. That didn't mean leaving Marcus's memory behind. It meant living her life alongside it.

She pushed the pall of sadness off her shoulders with a final, desperate shove and said, "Let's go to Florida."

His arm tightened around her as she wiped the remaining tears from her cheeks. The corded muscles made her feel safe and cared for. He laid a gentle kiss on the back of her head and whispered, "I'd like that…"

"Promise me something?" she asked, squirming from his grasp and pulling some tissues from the box he kept on this side of the bed just for her. He'd seen her at her worst more than once, but until now, she'd never been self-conscious about blowing her nose in front of him. She succeeded with minimal grossness.

"All right…"

Spooning back into his warmth, she gave him a half-hearted elbow. "Update the algorithm and AI. No more effing squirrels, or wildlife of any kind."

Chuckling softly, he moved her hair aside and kissed the delicate skin at the base of her neck. "I promise that and a whole lot more…if you'll let me."

The touch of his lips sent a shiver far and wide, awakening long-dormant bits of her anatomy. She smiled in the dark and whispered, "I'll consider it."

He gave her another squeeze. "That's all I ask. Sleep now, Livvie. Tomorrow's a new day." He found her hand and threaded his fingers through hers. "We'll face it together, all right?"

For once, the thought gave her a thrill. Her body relaxed against Bach, the only place she wanted to be. Content, she drifted off to sleep, and for the first time in five years, she looked forward to what tomorrow might bring.

Want more?

Dear Readers,

Thank you so much for reading *PERFECT ODDS*! I hope you enjoyed Liv, Bach, Tanya, and Tate's stories.

Looking for more? Consider my award-winning *CAUGHT UP IN LOVE* trilogy. A unique blend of contemporary romance and women's fiction, the novels center around three New Jersey women: romance writer Jillian Grant; her sister, Kitty; and Kitty's daughter, Jenny. All will tug at your heartstrings as they find redemption and surrender their hearts for a second chance at love. Turn the page for brief book descriptions, or download free samples here:

Caught Up in Raine   Surrender My Heart

Consider leaving a review on Amazon, Goodreads, or sharing on Instagram or TikTok (#BookTok). Please and thank you! I'd love to hear from you. Connect on my website, lgoconnor (dot) com, Instagram @lg_oconnor, and if you're into health & wellness, substack.lgoconnor.com.

Warmest Regards,

~L.G.

Get Caught Up in the Caught Up in Love series

CAUGHT UP IN RAINE (Novel)
Two hearts. One soul-shattering decision. Plagued by loss, bestselling romance author, Jillian Grant, enlists a young landscaper with an uncanny resemblance to the boyfriend she lost at eighteen—and the male lead in her next novel—as her cover model. When Raine ends up in the hospital with no place to go, Jillian offers him a place to stay until sparks ignite, giving Jillian more than she bargained for and forcing her to confront the past that she has tried to forget.

REDISCOVERING RAINE (A Caught Up in Raine Novelette)
Two hearts. One magical night. Pick up where we left off in CAUGHT UP IN RAINE from Raine's point-of-view and experience his magical night with Jillian. But putting a ring on Jillian's finger doesn't mean all is easily forgiven.

CAUGHT UP IN RACHEL (A Caught Up In Raine Novelette)
Two hearts. One small miracle. Giving birth at an "advanced maternal age" isn't without peril, as Jillian discovers when she develops a condition that threatens mother and child.

SHELTER MY HEART (Novel)
Two weeks. One life-changing proposal. Devon, an ailing young CEO persuades Jenny, an engaged, young woman to accept a two-week proposal: spend her vacation with him and attend his family's society gala so they can convince the Board of Directors that he's healthy and going to marry to fulfil the terms of his inheritance and save his family. No strings. No future. Until the stakes rise, forcing Jenny to choose between her heart and saving Devon's life.

SURRENDER MY HEART (Novel)

Two old flames. One new destiny. Kitty McNally knows sometimes you need to make the best of the worst choices for the ones you love. Ever since their high school breakup, Kitty McNally has secretly loved Detective John Henshaw. The hardest thing she'd ever done was leave him behind—not once, but twice. Decades later, a hint of what they had still shines in his eyes. But only the dead know the secrets she still keeps. At their 35th High School reunion, Kitty has one last chance to confront the past and rekindle their love—if John can forgive her once he learns the truth.

Praise for the Caught Up in Love Series

"O'Connor's contemporary romance is very realistic and will tug on the heartstrings of probably more readers than she expected...Jillian and Raine have faced a lifetime's worth of secrets and heartbreaks...you'll want to cheer them on until the very end." ~**RT Book Reviews**

"The plot is driven by a May-December premise that is blown away in the sexy love scenes." ~**Library Journal**

"For all the contemporary romance fans out there, this book is for you." ~**Night Owl Reviews**

"Urban fantasy author O'Connor (Trinity Stones) branches out into romantic women's fiction with a sexy tale of angst, guilt, love, and hate." ~**Publishers Weekly**

"LG O'Connor had me at "hello" with this plot. Phenomenal writing skills at work is what has made Caught Up in Raine a hard to beat Romance for 2016..." ~**HEA Romances with a Little Kick Blog**

"This story is both beautiful and haunting...I loved every second of this sexy, sweet and romantic book!!!" ~**The Romance Reviews, Top Pick, 5 stars**

"O'Connor delivers a unique women's fiction story packed with emotion, humor and sexiness. I could not turn the pages quickly enough…" ~**Caridad Pineiro,** *NY Times & USA Today* **Bestselling Romance Author**

"WOW! What an absolutely fantastic story! I absolutely fell in love with Raine, and wanted Jillian for a girlfriend! Well written and very relevant as a contemporary romance with two amazing, memorable characters." ~**Carla Susan Smith, Author of A Vampire's Promise**

"A well-polished, wonderfully written love story driven by believable characters whose strengths and flaws add complexity to a fairy-tale romance." ~**IndieReader, 4.5 stars**

About the Author

Photo credit: Oak & Ivy Photography

L.G. O'Connor writes romantic women's fiction, paranormal, and suspense that touches the heart with themes of family, redemption, forgiveness, and most of all, hope. She's the author of the multi-award-winning romantic women's fiction trilogy: *Caught Up in Raine, Shelter My Heart,* and *Surrender My Heart*, which follows a family of three New Jersey women who must confront ghosts of the past to find redemption and second chances. Besides writing, L.G. is a Mayo Clinic & Board-Certified Wellness Coach. She's passionate about connecting with readers and loves food, antiques, and excellent coffee.

Find her books or stay in touch:

Website	Amazon	Bookbub
Goodreads	Instagram	Substack